Clarion Books
a Houghton Mifflin Company imprint
215 Park Avenue South, New York, NY 10003
Copyright © 2002 by l'école des loisirs
Originally published in France in 2002 under the title *La chaussette verte de Lisette*.
First American edition, 2005.

The illustrations were executed in watercolors.
The text was set in 15-point GillSans Bold.

www.houghtonmifflinbooks.com

Manufactured in China.

Library of Congress Cataloging-in-Publication Data
Valckx, Catharina.
 [Chausette verte de Lisette. English]
 Lizette's green sock / by Catharina Valckx.—1st American ed.
     p. cm.
Originally published in France in 2002 under title: La chaussette verte de Lisette.
Summary: Lizette tries to figure out what to do with the one green sock that she
finds while out walking one day.
ISBN 0-618-45298-2
[1. Socks—Fiction.] I. Title.
PZ7.V213Ch 2005
[E]—dc22   2004012042

ISBN-13: 978-0-618-45298-9
ISBN-10: 0-618-45298-2

LEO 10 9 8 7 6 5 4 3 2 1

Lizette's Green Sock

by Catharina Valckx

Clarion Books • New York

It's a beautiful sunny day,
and Lizette is going for a walk.

She hasn't gone far when she finds a sock.
A pretty green sock.

4

"I'm lucky," says Lizette. "You don't find a
beautiful sock like this every day!" She puts it on
and goes happily on her way.

Soon she comes upon Tim and Tom, brothers who love
to tease her. "Look what I found!" she announces proudly.
But the brothers make fun of her. "One sock! What a
dummy! Where's the other one? Socks come in pairs!"

"That's right," says Lizette. "They do come
in pairs. Well, I'll have to find the other one."

Lizette climbs the tallest tree. From the top she can see everything. But no matter how hard she squints, she doesn't see even the shadow of a sock.

"I know!" she exclaims. "It fell in the pond. That's why I can't see it." She climbs down quickly and runs toward the pond.

Lizette dunks her head into the cold water.
Fortunately, a fish is swimming by. Maybe he can help her.

"Hello, Mr. Fish. Have you seen a sock?"

"No," says the fish. "But look at this. I found a huge
watering can and a black comb. Isn't it amazing, all the
stuff that falls into the water?"

"Yes," sighs Lizette. "But I'm looking for a sock."

Disappointed, Lizette returns home.

"Why are you so sad, sweetie?" asks Mama.
"I found a sock," Lizette tells her. "But
one sock doesn't count. It has to be a pair."

"That's right," says Mama. "Socks come in pairs, just like shoes. Give it to me and I'll wash it. You can't wear a sock you found on the ground. It's dirty."

Lizette sits and waits for her sock to dry.

"Is that your cap?"

Lizette turns and sees her friend Bert.

"It isn't a cap," she tells him. "It's a sock."

"It *is?*" Bert is amazed. "You know, I've always dreamed of having a cap like that. May I try it on?"

"If you want."

Lizette bursts out laughing. "My sock looks great on you!"

"You see," says Bert, "it's a super cap."

"You're right," says Lizette. "If I had two, I'd give one to you."

Tim and Tom come sneaking around the corner of the house. "Yoo hoo!" calls Tim. "Look what we found, Lizette—the second sock!"

"Where was it?" exclaims Lizette.
But instead of answering, the brothers run away,
shouting, "Come and get your sock!"
Lizette and Bert take off in pursuit.

"Whew! They're small, but they're fast," gasps Tom.

"But they won't get their sock," Tim says with a nasty laugh. "And . . . splash!"

24

Lizette and Bert arrive out of breath.
"Come on," says Lizette. "Give us the sock now."
"What sock? We don't have a sock anymore.
Look! It flew away."

Bert leads the way back to Lizette's house.
"Forget it," he tells her. "They're mean, and
what's more, they're liars. Socks can't fly."

"What a mess," says Lizette. "Now we won't have another cap. But you can keep mine for a while if you want. You can give it back to me at home."

"That's nice of you," says Bert in a small voice.

At home there is a surprise waiting. Lizette's
mama has knitted a new sock. A green one!
Exactly like the other one! Lizette jumps for
joy and kisses her mama.

"You're going to wear it on your head?" Mama asks, perplexed. "Like Bert?"

"Yes, that's the best way!" Lizette explains. "Because now we both have a super cap. A pair of caps!"

Bert is so delighted he does a little dance.

29

Bert has gone home. It's bedtime. Lizette
happily gets into bed with her cap on.

She thinks about her friend. He's happily
sleeping with his cap on, too. Lizette is sure he is.

But happiest of all is the fish. Because now he has
not only a black comb and a huge watering can,
he also has a splendid sleeping bag.